To my big and wonderful extended family who, through their prayers, giving and support, demonstrate that there is nothing more important in life than loving God and each other—not just at our marvelous Christmas gatherings, but all year long!

–R.O.

To Tabita, Louie, Lila, Timmy and Pete.

Merry Christmases always!

–J.G.

The Legend of the CHRISTMAS STOCKING

Written by
Rick Osborne

Illustrated by
Jim Griffin

ZONDERVAN.com/
AUTHORTRACKER
follow your favorite authors

New *York Evening Post!* Get it here!" Peter waved his last newspaper. "Read all about it. Pirates on the high seas!" A stagecoach rolled up and stopped. A man leaned out and said, "I'll take that, Peter. Any word about your father?"

"No, sir, but we expect his ship to return soon." Peter thanked the man, put the coins in his pocket, and started to run. He had an important stop to make before going home.

Peter stopped in front of a small shop, slicked back his hair, and stomped the frozen snow off his boots. A sign hanging above the window of the store read, "Everything Wood." Peter looked inside and his heart sank.

Bursting into the store, he said, "Mr. Dewey, where is it? You didn't sell it did you?"

Jim Dewey looked up and laughed. The woodworker was a long-time family friend. He was old enough to be Peter's grandfather, but his cheery smile made him seem a lot younger. "Slow down, Pete! You know you can call me Uncle Jim."

"Sorry, Uncle Jim, I was just worried. So where is the ship?"

Uncle Jim brushed wood shavings from his leather apron. Reaching up to a top shelf, he took down a big model ship. He carefully set it on the wooden counter. Peter sucked in his breath. "This is an exact copy of the *U.S.S. Constitution*—the pride of the squadron. It's a three-masted, 204-foot frigate. It's almost identical to the one your dad is sailing on. You didn't really think I would sell it to someone else, did you?" Uncle Jim teased.

"I didn't know. Why did you take it out of the window and hang up some old socks instead?" Peter asked.

Uncle Jim laughed. "The stockings are for Christmas presents."

"Who'd want socks for Christmas?" Peter asked.

"Not as a present! They hold presents. You know, lemon drops for your sisters…chocolates for your mother…" Jim said.

Peter gave Jim a funny smile. "I don't know if I'd want lemon drops after they'd been in one of my socks. And this schooner would never fit."

"Peter," Jim said slowly. "What will you do if your dad doesn't get back in time for Christmas? Would you be willing to use the money you've saved for this ship to buy Christmas presents for your family?"

Peter swallowed hard. "My dad will be back."

"I hope so," Uncle Jim said, reaching for his coat. "Would you like a ride home? It's a long way in the snow."

Peter nodded.

Peter's mother looked up from her sewing just as he carried a load of wood through the kitchen door. "How did you do today, son?"

"Sold every paper, except yours, of course. Everyone knows we're waiting for Dad to come home, so they all buy papers from me."

Peter set down the wood just as his youngest sister, Patricia, skidded through the room and hugged him. He smelled the beef stew that his sister Christa was cooking for dinner.

After putting two coins into his pouch, he handed the rest of his week's pay to his mother. His stomach growled as he thought about eating the stew.

Mother, any word about Dad? The newspaper says our fleet is having trouble with pirates," asked Peter.

"It's fine, Peter, I'm sure it is just a bad winter storm," Mother assured him.

"Uncle Jim said if Dad doesn't get home in time, I should give you the money I have to buy gifts for the girls. But I really want that schooner!"

She sighed. "I know. But how would your sisters feel on Christmas morning if you have that beautiful boat and the girls only have an apple and a piece of candy?"

"But I deserve it. I'm the one doing all the work! Dad said if I worked while he was away I could use some of the money I earned to buy the boat." Peter choked back his tears. "I just want him to come home."

His mother hugged him. "I know, I miss him too."

Pastor Spring took his spot behind the podium. Smiling, he said, "For those of you wondering about my socks, don't worry, they're clean." Everyone laughed. Pastor Spring's eyes sparkled as he looked around the room. "I've hung up my best pair of socks because I want to tell you about the tradition of hanging socks or stockings on the fireplace mantle on Christmas Eve. Perhaps you've already read about hanging up socks in Peter's *New York Evening Post*." Peter grinned.

Pastor Spring continued, "But where did we ever get such an idea? Let me tell you the story."

The church went quiet. Everyone liked Pastor Spring's stories.

It started many, many years ago with a poor man I'll call Stephanas. He was a shoemaker. One day, he was putting the final touches on a very fine pair of sandals when the door of his shop squeaked open and a well-dressed young man stepped in. "I trust that you and your daughters are well?" the young man said.

"I am fine, Nicholas," Stephanas replied. "I only have one worry in life."

"And what is that?" Nicholas asked.

"My daughters want to be married," Stephanas said. "I don't know if I'll be able to afford three dowries."

"Hmm," Nicholas said. "Without the dowry money, your girls can never be married. Is that right?"

Stephanas nodded his head sadly.

"God will help!" Nicholas told the old man.

"I hope you are right," Stephanas replied. Nicholas paid for his shoes and left.

A few nights later, Stephanas and his daughters were sitting by the fireplace after dinner when something heavy flew through the open window and landed *CLINK!* on the stone floor. Stephanas and his three daughters gasped. Claudia, the oldest girl, ran to pick it up.

"Father, someone has given us a bag of gold coins!" said Claudia.

"Now you can be married, Claudia!" their father rejoiced. The three sisters laughed and danced around the room. Stephanas ran to the window to see who had been so generous. The street was empty.

Soon after Claudia's wedding, a second bag of gold flew through the window and landed *CLINK!* on the floor. "It must be for you, Tryphena!" the youngest daughter Phoebe said. Again Stephanas looked outside, but again he found no one.

One damp evening, some time after the second wedding, Phoebe hung her washing around the room to dry. She hung her socks over the fireplace. Would you believe it? A third leather pouch filled with gold flew in through the open window. But this time, the gold landed in one of Phoebe's stockings!

Stephanas rushed out the door and ran after the unknown giver. "Stop!" he called. "Why are you doing this?" Then Stephanas saw someone in the darkness, and he knew who it was. "Nicholas? Is that you? Please stop, Nicholas!"

Nicholas stepped out of the darkness. He wanted his gifts to be a secret.

"Before my parents died, they gave me three bags of gold. They wanted me to have enough for everything I needed. But when you told me about your daughters, I knew I had to help."

"But you gave us all three bags of gold! And we did nothing to deserve them!" Stephanas cried.

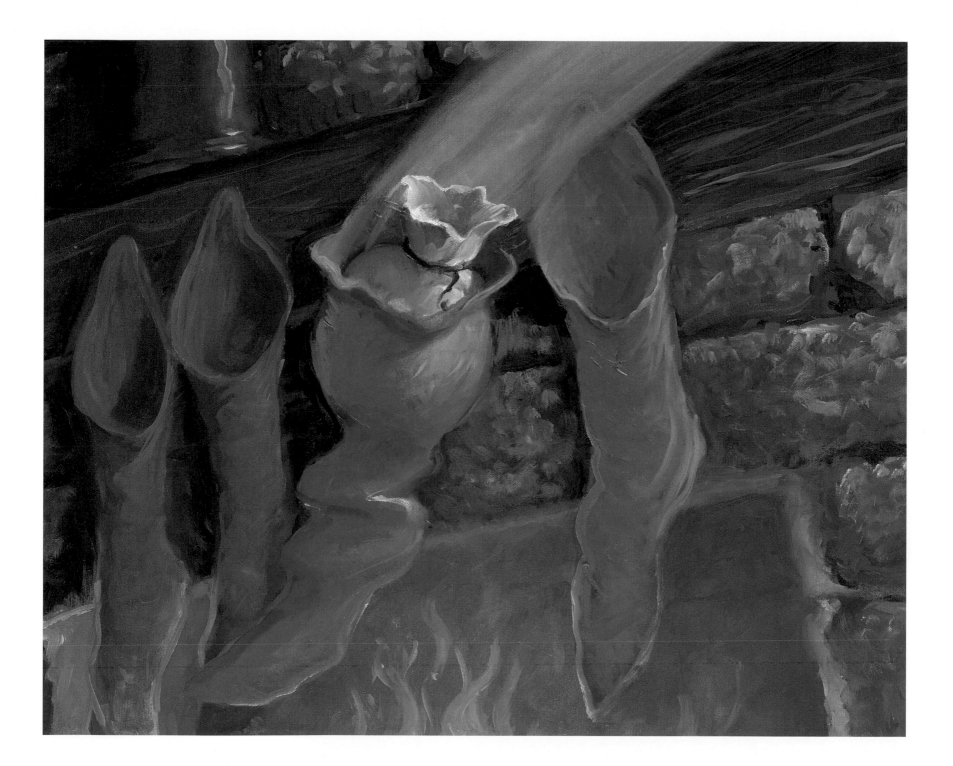

Nicholas served God," Pastor Spring explained. "He understood that God had set the example for giving when he gave his only Son, Jesus. None of us deserved to have Jesus die for us. As God gives to us even when we don't deserve it, giving to others shows God's love."

Peter hung his head and thought of his leather pouch of money. Pastor Spring went on.

"As the years went by, the story of the gift of gold spread, and people started to hang stockings by the fireplace on a special day each year. Now people here in New York are starting to hang stockings on Christmas Eve. I can't think of a better way to remind us all of God's wonderful gift to us: Jesus."

Peter prayed. He asked God to help him be more generous and whispered aloud: "Please bring my dad home safely."

Every night Mother secretly sewed special stockings as a surprise for Peter and his sisters. She stitched each child's name along the top.

On Christmas morning Peter watched with joy as his sisters emptied their stockings, giggling and squealing at the contents. Each had an apple, a leather pouch of lemon drops, and a beautiful hand-carved wooden doll.

The girls hugged their mother. "Give Peter a hug too! He worked very hard to buy us all presents so that we could have a happy Christmas." Peter couldn't stop smiling. What he had done felt so right.

He handed his mother a beautifully wrapped package. "This is for you," Peter said. Tears filled his mother's eyes as she opened the gift. It was his mother's favorite chocolates—the ones Peter's dad usually bought her for Christmas. Inside was a small card. It read: "I miss him too. Peter."

Knock, knock, knock. Peter ran to open the door. There stood Uncle Jim.

"Merry Christmas!" Uncle Jim said, smiling. "I brought you something."

Just then a man stepped out from behind Uncle Jim. *"Dad!"* They hugged each other and Peter wouldn't let go. The rest of the family crowded around and joined in the hugging.

Later, when everyone was settled around the crackling fire, Dad said to Peter, "I was so eager to see you all, I didn't bring my bags inside. Would you go get them out of Jim's wagon?"

"Sure, Dad." Peter ran to the small, horse-drawn wagon and stopped dead in his tracks. He started to whoop. There in the wagon was the wooden schooner. It looked even bigger and more beautiful than Peter remembered!

His dad walked up and put an arm around Peter. "I'm proud of you, Son." Peter smiled and thought of how glad he was that the story of the stockings had reminded him what Christmas is all about.

THE LEGEND OF THE CHRISTMAS STOCKING began in present-day Turkey about 300 hundred years after Jesus was born. The exact details of the story have been lost, but legend tells us that Nicholas anonymously gave three bags of gold to a man whose daughters could not get married because he had no dowry. The last bag of gold reportedly landed in the youngest daughter's stocking. Thus the tradition of putting gifts in stockings began.

Nicholas served God his entire life. His many generous deeds demonstrated God's love and inspired people everywhere to give unselfishly.

Slowly over a period of time his name and appearance changed. In England, Saint Nicholas became Father Christmas. Today we call him Santa Claus, which came from the Dutch name for Saint Nicholas, Sinterklaas. In the early 1800s, the time of our story, placing gifts in stockings was moved from Saint Nicholas Eve, December 6, and became part of our Christmas celebration.

Behind the legends that the real Saint Nicholas inspired was the true meaning of Christmas: God gave us his only Son because he loves us. God wants us to show his love by giving to others and caring for them.

The Legend of the Christmas Stocking. Copyright ©2004 by Lightwave Publishing, Inc. Illustrations copyright © 2004 by Jim Griffin

Requests for information should be addressed to: Zonderkidz, Grand Rapids, MI 49530

Library of Congress Cataloging-in-Publication Data
Osborne, Rick.
  Legend of the Christmas stocking : an inspirational story of a wish come true / written by Rick Osborne ; illustrated by Jim Griffin.-- 1st ed.
     p. cm.
  Summary: With his father away at sea, it is up to Peter to help make sure his mother and sisters have a merry Christmas. Includes brief notes on Santa Claus and the legendary origin of the Christmas stocking.
  ISBN 0-310-70898-2 (hardcover)
  [1. Christmas--Fiction. 2. Family life--Fiction. 3. Conduct of life--Fiction.] I. Griffin, Jim, 1949- ill. II. Title.
PZ7.O8125Le 2004
[E]--dc22
                              2004000339

Editor: Gwen Ellis. Art Direction: Laura M. Maitner.

Printed in China. 13 14 • 13 12